Withdrawn

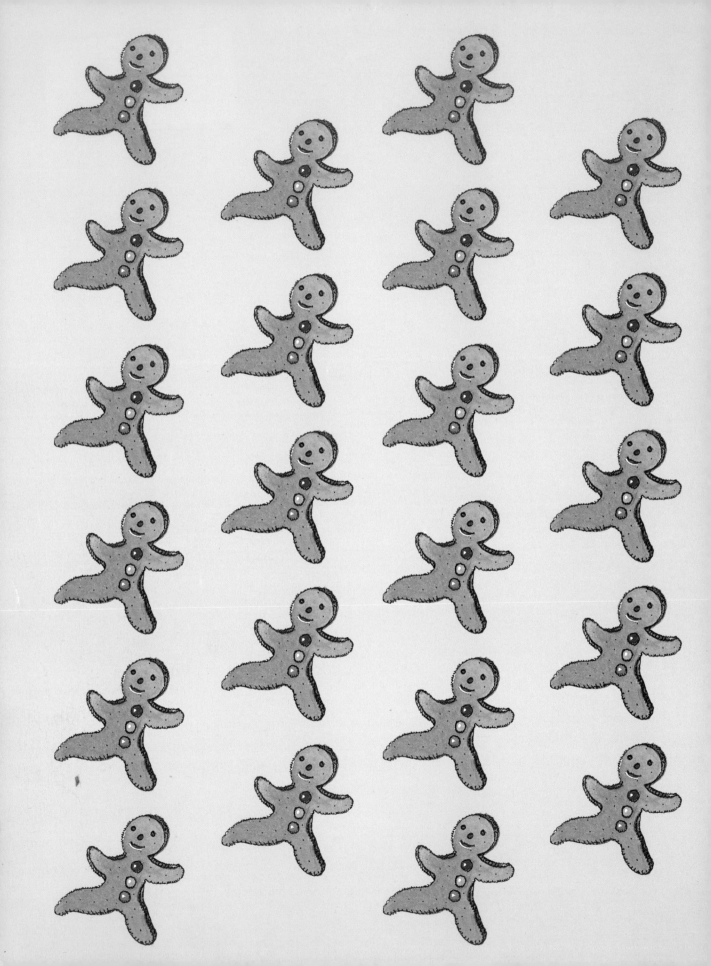

OXFORD
UNIVERSITY PRESS

Great Clarendon Street, Oxford OX2 6DP

Oxford University Press is a department of the University of Oxford.
It furthers the University's objective of excellence in research, scholarship,
and education by publishing worldwide in

Oxford   New York

Auckland   Cape Town   Dar es Salaam   Hong Kong   Karachi
Kuala Lumpur   Madrid   Melbourne   Mexico City   Nairobi
New Delhi   Shanghai   Taipei   Toronto

With offices in

Argentina   Austria   Brazil   Chile   Czech Republic   France   Greece
Guatemala   Hungary   Italy   Japan   Poland   Portugal   Singapore
South Korea   Switzerland   Thailand   Turkey   Ukraine   Vietnam

Oxford is a registered trade mark of Oxford University Press
in the UK and in certain other countries

British Library Cataloguing in Publication Data

Data available

ISBN: 978-0-19-272539-4 (paperback)

9 10 8

Printed in Hong Kong

Paper used in the production of this book is a natural,
recyclable product made from wood grown in sustainable forests.
The manufacturing process conforms to the environmental
regulations of the country of origin.

The
GINGERBREAD
BOY

IAN BECK

OXFORD
UNIVERSITY PRESS

Once upon a time and a long time ago, there lived an old man and an old woman. They had no children of their own, so one morning the old woman decided to make them a little boy out of gingerbread.

She put two raisins for his eyes, and one for his nose, and three little candy buttons on his front.

'What a fine boy,' said her husband, and they popped him in the oven to bake.

When he was ready, they opened the oven door and out he jumped. He ran across the kitchen and out through the open door.

The old couple chased after him, calling out, 'Stop, stop, come back, you're our little gingerbread boy.'

'Stop, stop, come back, you're

our little gingerbread boy.'

But the little gingerbread boy ran on, with his cheeky smile, and he called back to them: 'Run, run, as fast as you can. You can't catch me, I'm the gingerbread man.'

'Run, run as fast as you can.

You can't catch me, I'm the gingerbread man.'

And the poor old man and old woman really couldn't run fast enough to catch him.

On and on ran the little gingerbread boy,
out of the town and into the fields, until
he met a cow.

'Moo,' said the cow. 'Stop, little gingerbread boy. I want to eat you all up.'

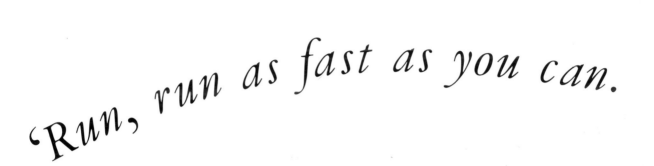

'Run, run as fast as you can.

But the little gingerbread boy ran on. 'I can run faster than the old man and the old woman, and I can run faster than you.

'Run, run, as fast as you can. You can't catch me, I'm the gingerbread man.'

And the cow couldn't run fast enough to catch him.

You can't catch me, I'm the gingerbread man.'

On and on, even faster, ran the little
gingerbread boy, until he met a horse.

'Neigh,' said the horse. 'Stop, little
gingerbread boy. I want to eat you all up.'
But the little gingerbread boy
ran on.

'Run, run as fast as you can.

'I can run faster than the old man and the old woman, and the cow, and I can run faster than you.

'Run, run, as fast as you can. You can't catch me, I'm the gingerbread man.'

You can't catch me, I'm the gingerbread man.'

And even the horse wasn't fast enough to catch him.

On and on, faster and faster, ran the little gingerbread boy, until he met a farmer.

'Hey, you!' called the farmer. 'Stop, little gingerbread boy. You're just what I'd like for my tea.'

'Run, run as fast as you can. You can't catch me,

But the little gingerbread boy ran on. 'I can run faster than the old man and the old woman, and the cow, and the horse, and I can run faster than you.

'Run, run, as fast as you can. You can't catch me, I'm the gingerbread man.'

And the farmer couldn't run fast enough to catch him.

I'm the gingerbread man.'

On and on ran the little gingerbread boy,
until he came to a river. And there he met a
clever, hungry fox.

'Why don't I help you, little gingerbread
boy?' said the fox. 'Hop on my tail, and I'll
swim you over to the other side.'

So the little gingerbread boy jumped on to
the fox's tail, and together they set off.

After a while, the fox said, 'You seem to
be getting wet. Why not jump further up my
back?'

So the little gingerbread boy jumped up
on to the fox's back.

When they were halfway across, the fox said,
'You're getting heavy. Why not hop up on to
my nose?'

So the little gingerbread boy hopped up
on to the fox's nose.

But when they reached the other side of
the river the fox turned his head, snapped
open his mouth, and, *crunch*, half the little
gingerbread boy was gone.

'Oh dear,' said the little gingerbread boy.

Then, *crunch*, went the fox's jaws again, and the little gingerbread boy, with his cheeky grin, was all gone.

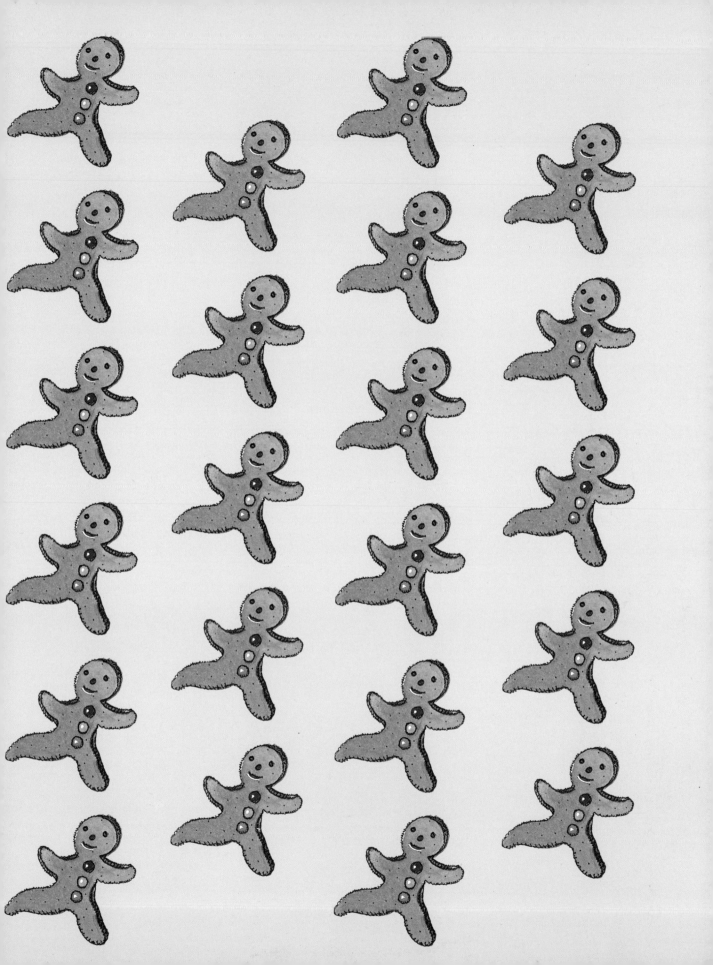